World of Reading

W9-BNW-513

JOURNEY TO STAR WARS: THE LAST JEDI

STAR WARS™

A LEADER NAMED LEIA

WRITTEN BY JENNIFER HEDDLE
ART BY BRIAN ROOD

Disney
LUCASFILM
PRESS
LOS ANGELES · NEW YORK

All rights reserved. Published by Disney • Lucasfilm Press, an imprint
of Disney Book Group. No part of this book may be reproduced or
transmitted in any form or by any means, electronic or mechanical,
including photocopying, recording, or by any information storage and
retrieval system, without written permission from the publisher. For
information address Disney • Lucasfilm Press, 1101 Flower Street, Glendale,
California 91201.

Printed in the United States of America

First Edition, September 2017   10 9 8 7 6 5 4 3 2

Library of Congress Control Number on file

FAC-029261-17272

ISBN 978-1-368-00976-8

Visit the official *Star Wars* website at: www.starwars.com.

There once was a princess named Leia.

Leia was strong and brave.

She fought for what was right.

She was a rebel.

The evil Empire did not like rebels.
The Imperials wanted
to control the galaxy.
They built a weapon
called the Death Star.

The Death Star
could destroy whole planets.
But Princess Leia had
the secret plans to the Death Star.
The rebels could use the plans to
stop the evil Empire.

The Imperial leader Darth Vader
captured Princess Leia's ship.
Leia needed to hide
the Death Star plans.
She gave the plans
to a droid named R2-D2.

When Darth Vader asked for the plans,
Princess Leia lied.
She said she did not know
where the plans were.
But the evil Empire would not
let her go until they found the plans.

R2-D2 gave the plans to
Luke Skywalker and Han Solo.
Luke and Han tried to rescue Leia.
But Leia had to rescue
Luke and Han instead!

Princess Leia gave the
plans to the rebels.
The rebels blew up the Death Star!
Leia, Luke, and Han were heroes.
But the evil Empire was still powerful.

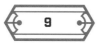

Princess Leia and the rebels
built a new secret base.
The rebel base was on
the frozen planet Hoth.
Hoth was very cold.

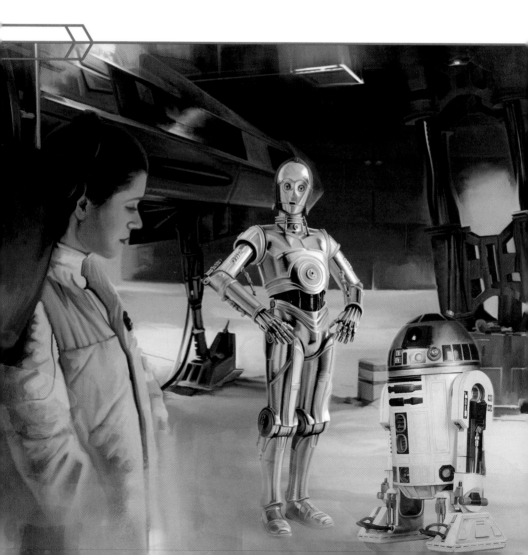

The evil Empire
found the rebel base on Hoth!
The rebels had to leave.
Princess Leia left Hoth
with Han Solo.
Darth Vader chased them!

Leia and Han flew to Cloud City.
Han's friend Lando lived in Cloud City.
Han trusted Lando.
Lando would help them
escape from Darth Vader.

But Lando did not help them.
Instead, Lando turned Leia
and Han over to Darth Vader!

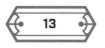

Vader froze Han in carbonite and sent him to an alien named Jabba the Hutt.
Princess Leia was sad.
She loved Han Solo.

Luke and Leia escaped from
Darth Vader and went back
to the rebels.
Then they came up with
a plan to rescue Han!

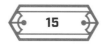

Leia pretended to be a bounty
hunter and snuck into Jabba's palace.
Then Luke arrived!
Together, they saved Han Solo.

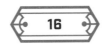

Leia even defeated Jabba the Hutt!
But the rebels still had not
defeated the evil Empire.

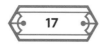

Leia, Luke, and Han had a new mission.
They flew to the forest moon of Endor.
They needed to destroy the
shield that protected
the Empire's new Death Star!

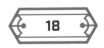

Leia and Luke rode on speeder bikes through the forest.
Imperial stormtroopers chased them!
Leia crashed.
The troopers were going to capture her!

But Princess Leia met
an Ewok named Wicket.
Wicket helped Leia escape
from the troopers.
Then Wicket took Leia
to his Ewok village.

The Ewoks had found Luke, Han,
Chewie, and C-3PO!
Leia was glad to see her friends.
Then Leia learned that
Luke was her brother!
Leia was happy.

The Ewoks helped the rebels destroy
the shield that protected
the new Death Star.
The rebels blew up the Death Star
and defeated the Empire!
Everyone was happy!

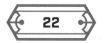

Years later, Leia and Han Solo had
a son named Ben.
But Ben turned to the
dark side of the Force.
Ben became Kylo Ren.
Kylo Ren helped the evil First Order.

The evil First Order wanted to
be like the evil Empire.
They even built a weapon
like the Death Star.
But the Starkiller was
much larger than the Death Star.

Leia wanted to stop the evil First Order.
She became a general.
General Leia led the Resistance
against the First Order.

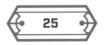

Leia needed help from her friends
to stop the First Order.
Leia asked Han Solo
to stop Kylo Ren.

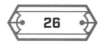

Han Solo was brave.

He helped destroy the Starkiller.

But he could not stop Kylo Ren.

Leia needed her brother's help.
But Luke was missing.
Leia asked her new friend Rey
to find Luke.

The First Order grew
stronger every day.
Kylo Ren would not rest until
he had defeated the Resistance.
Leia needed to keep the Resistance safe
while she waited for Luke and Rey.

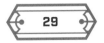

But Leia was not alone.
Leia trusted her droid, C-3PO.

Admiral Ackbar was
also by Leia's side.

Admiral Holdo
would help Leia, too.

And Poe Dameron
was Leia's best pilot.
Together they would
keep the Resistance safe.

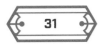

Princess or general,
Leia has always been strong and brave.
And she will always fight
for what is right.
Leia is a leader.
Leia is a rebel.

PRINCESS LEIA

© LFL